KIT

D14105579

School for Sillies

by JAY WILLIAMS *with pictures by* FRISO HENSTRA

Parents' Magazine Press · New York

Printed in the United States of America
Library of Congress Catalog Card Number: 71-77785

Other books by Jay Williams

The Practical Princess
The King with Six Friends
The Cookie Tree
The Question Box
Philbert the Fearful
To Catch a Bird
co-author of the Danny Dunn *books*

Some kings are proud of their riches, and some of their power, but King Kilian was proud because he was the smartest man in the kingdom. Some people might not be certain of such a thing, but King Kilian was certain for several reasons.

In the first place, nobody ever contradicted him. If he said a thing was so, everyone said, "Yes, Your Majesty."

When he sat in the great throne room and judged the problems his subjects brought him, nobody disagreed with his decisions.

All his courtiers said, "Your Majesty is certainly the wisest man in the kingdom."

All the colleges gave him honorary degrees, so that he was a Doctor of Law, Doctor of Philosophy, and Doctor of Tree Surgery. He was also Commander of the Army, and Lord of the High, Low, and Middle Justice. He felt sure that being all these things made him much smarter than anyone else, and he had medals and diplomas and titles to prove it.

OCTOR OF LAW
TOR OF PHILOS
ERS
COMMANDER
OF THE ARMY
OCTOR OF MUSIC
REE SURGERY
LORD
NG
LORD
LORD
OG PROTA
RICULTURE
TECTURE
OOKING

His daughter, Zinnia, was naturally the smartest girl in the kingdom. King Kilian knew this was so because he himself had said it.

"Therefore," said he, "she must marry someone who will fit into our family. She can only marry a man who is wiser than I am. And," he added, with a proud smile, "you have to get up pretty early in the morning to get the best of me."

One morning very early, before anyone else was up, a young man came strolling into the great city of Kilianistan. His shoes were dusty, his hands were deep in his pockets, and he was whistling merrily. His name was Kit.

He sauntered through quiet streets until he came to a pleasant square. Trees shaded it, and benches were set among flower beds. A high stone wall ran along one side. Kit sat down on a bench and took bread and cheese from his knapsack. He shared his breakfast with sparrows, who sang their thanks.

A church clock in the city chimed six. And somewhere, someone was sobbing bitterly. Listening carefully, Kit decided that the sound was coming from the other side of the wall. He pulled his bench close, climbed on its back, and with one spring was on top of the wall. He looked down into a splendid garden.

On the grass, a girl sat crying. Her beauty put the flowers to shame, and her tears were like drops of dew on the petals of a rose.

"Goodness!" said Kit. "What a sad noise for so fine a morning."

The girl lifted her face. "Who are you?" she asked.

Kit climbed down a thick vine and stood beside her. "I am a poor wandering scholar," he said. "I am studying the ways of the world."

"What have you found out?" the girl demanded.

"That it is wide and beautiful and lots of fun," Kit answered.

"Then you've learned only half of it," said the girl, scornfully. "For it is also full of trouble."

"What is your trouble?" Kit asked.

"My father is the wisest man in the kingdom," she said. "And so he will only allow me to marry someone wiser than he is. But no one can satisfy him, and I shall be unmarried until I die. Since he thinks I am the wisest girl in the kingdom, I have no friends and no sweethearts. No one is lonelier than I!"

“Dear me,” said Kit. “Your father must be a dreadful man.”
“If he heard you say that,” said Zinnia, “he would have your head chopped off. He is the king.”
‘I see,” Kit said, thoughtfully. “Well, dry your eyes and let us talk. For I have never heard of a trouble that could not be helped by friendship. I will be your friend.”

So they talked of this and that for a long time, and after a while Kit said, "And have you seen a man you want to marry?"

"I think I see him now," said Zinnia, shyly.

They kissed each other, and Kit said, "I will go and have a word with your father."

Off he went, and knocked at the main doors of the palace.

"I have come to try for the hand of the king's daughter," said he.

They looked him up and down, and let him sit in a corner until the king had finished his breakfast. Then, at last, the doors of the throne room were opened and Kit was shown inside. Minding his manners, he bowed low.

"Well, well, and what have we here?" said King Kilian. He put on his spectacles and looked fiercely at Kit. "I think I should warn you that my daughter has had three hundred and eighty-four suitors. And not one of them has satisfied me."

KING
KILIAN-NEWS

"Three hundred and eighty-five is my lucky number," said Kit.

"Humph! What do you do?" said the king.

"I am a wandering scholar," Kit replied.

"If you're still a scholar, then you don't yet know everything. That's a poor start," the king said. "Now I am a king. There's very little I don't know. Have you a college degree?"

"I'm a Bachelor of Arts."

"I," said the king, "am a Doctor of Literature, Doctor of Science, Doctor of Cooking, and too many others to mention. I am also descended from a long line of powerful and important rulers. What is your family?"

"My father is a poet, sir," said Kit.

"What?" shrieked the king, flying into a rage. "A poet? A nobody? A good-for-nothing writer of verses? Get out of my sight this instant! You can't even begin to satisfy me. All poets are fools, and the son of a poet must be a bigger fool than anyone else."

He clapped his hands. Two large guards came forward and picked up Kit. Gently but firmly they threw him through the doors of the throne room, the doors of the anteroom, and the doors of the palace, into the street.

Kit picked himself up. He dusted himself off. He looked in his purse. He had five gold pieces. "I think," he said, "that this is just enough. First, I must find some friends. And then, smart as the king is, perhaps there is something I can teach him."

The next morning, when King Kilian looked out of his window after breakfast, he saw across the street a large sign on the front of a house. SCHOOL FOR SILLIES, it said.

The king frowned. "That is something new," he muttered. "I must investigate it."

Wrapping himself in his cloak, he walked out and knocked loudly at the door of the house. Out came Kit, dressed in a long black robe and a tall black hat.

"Haven't I seen you somewhere before?" said the king, suspiciously.

"I don't think so, Your Majesty," Kit said. "I have been teaching for some time, but I have only just opened this branch of my school."

"A school for sillies? What on earth is it?" said the king.

"Your Majesty must know that most schools teach people how to be smart. But I teach them to be foolish."

"What's the good of that?" cried the king.

"I'm surprised at Your Majesty," Kit said. "You'll admit that there are more silly people than wise ones, won't you? That proves they must be of some good. And surely, if there were no foolish people, you would never know how wise you are."

The king pushed back his crown and scratched his head. "I never thought of it like that," he said.

"Silliness is an art," said Kit, solemnly. "Many people are born a little stupid. But to know how to be properly foolish must be learned. That is what my school is for. But perhaps," he added, "you would like to meet some of my more successful pupils. Then you would understand more fully what I mean."

"Very good!" said the king.

They walked together through the streets of the city and out of one of the gates into the countryside. They came to a house where, in the front yard, a man was standing with an umbrella over his head and an empty pail at his feet.

"Ah," Kit whispered to the king, "there is one of my pupils."

The king stared at the man. Then he said, "What are you doing?"

"Oh, good morning, Your Majesty," said the man. "I'm collecting sunshine."

"With an umbrella?"

"Well, my lord," the man explained, "my house is rather dark, so I tried gathering sunshine in pails. But when I brought them into the house, the sunshine, being very light, had floated out of the pails and escaped. Now, when this pail is full, I'll hold the umbrella over it and the sunshine will rise into the umbrella and be trapped there. Then I can shake it out in the house."

"I understand," said the king. And to Kit, he muttered, "This man seems to be a prize idiot."

At that instant, the man's wife, who had been mopping the floor upstairs, threw open an upper window and emptied a pail of dirty water. Down it splashed. Kit leaped aside, but the king was drenched. As for the silly, he stood calmly under his umbrella, quite dry.

"You see," said Kit, doing his best to dry the king's face with his handkerchief, "there are some advantages to real foolishness."

They walked on together. After a time, they came to a man sitting on a chair underneath a huge old tree. He held a fishing rod. The line rose up above his head and vanished among the leaves of the tree.

"Another pupil?" murmured the king.

Kit nodded.

"And what are you up to?" the king demanded of the man.

“Oh, good morning, Your Majesty,” the man said. “As you can see, I’m fishing.”

“In a tree?”

“Well, my lord,” said the man, “I am afraid of drowning, so I don’t go near the water. And I hate fish, so I am fishing for birds.”

“That makes a kind of peculiar sense,” said the king.

Before he could say anything else, the man began tugging at his line, yelling, "A bite! I've got a bite!" He gave the line a good pull, and down it came. On the hook was a roast chicken.

"That's a good morning's work," said the man, with satisfaction, and away he went.

The king stared after him, open-mouthed.

"You see," said Kit, "there are some rewards for being a real fool."

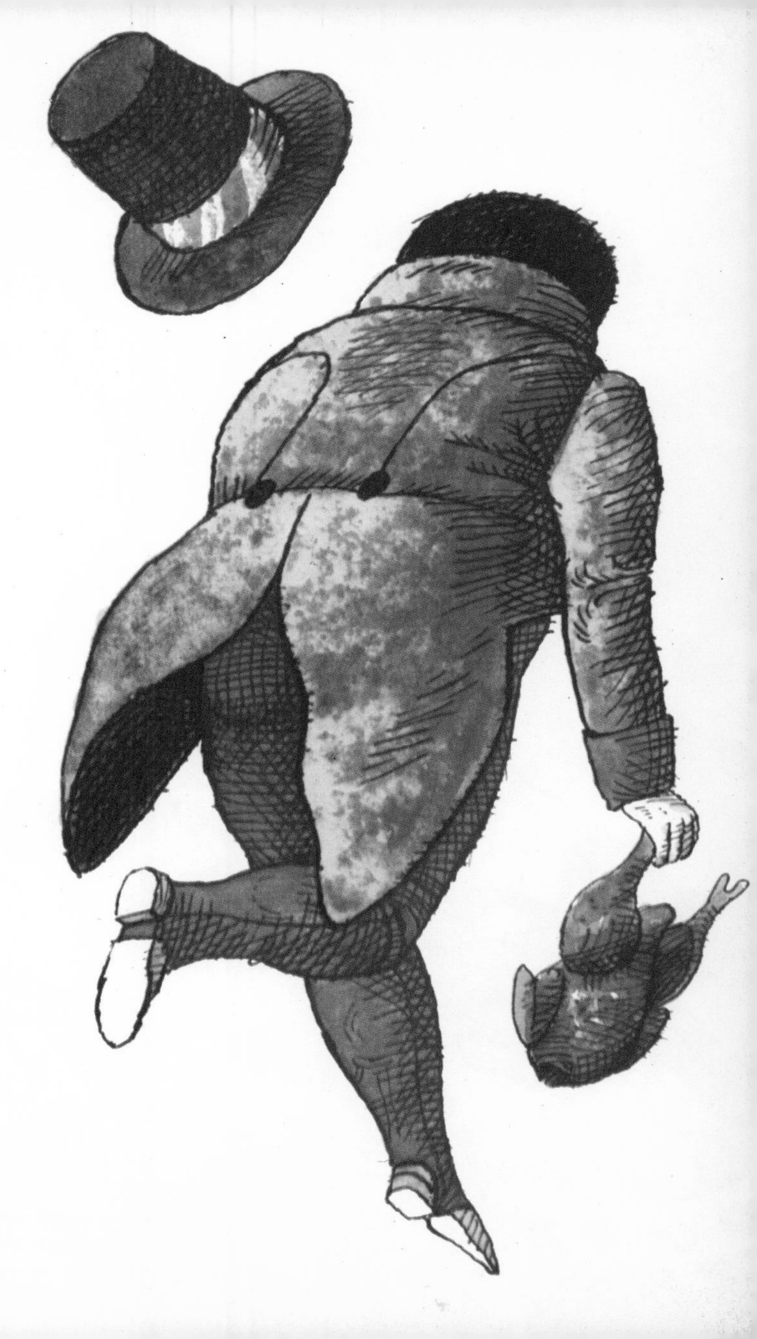

They walked on together. A little further on, they came to a man digging in a field.

"This man doesn't look like a silly," said the king.

"Ah, but he is one of my best pupils," Kit answered.

The king called out, "What are you doing, fellow?"

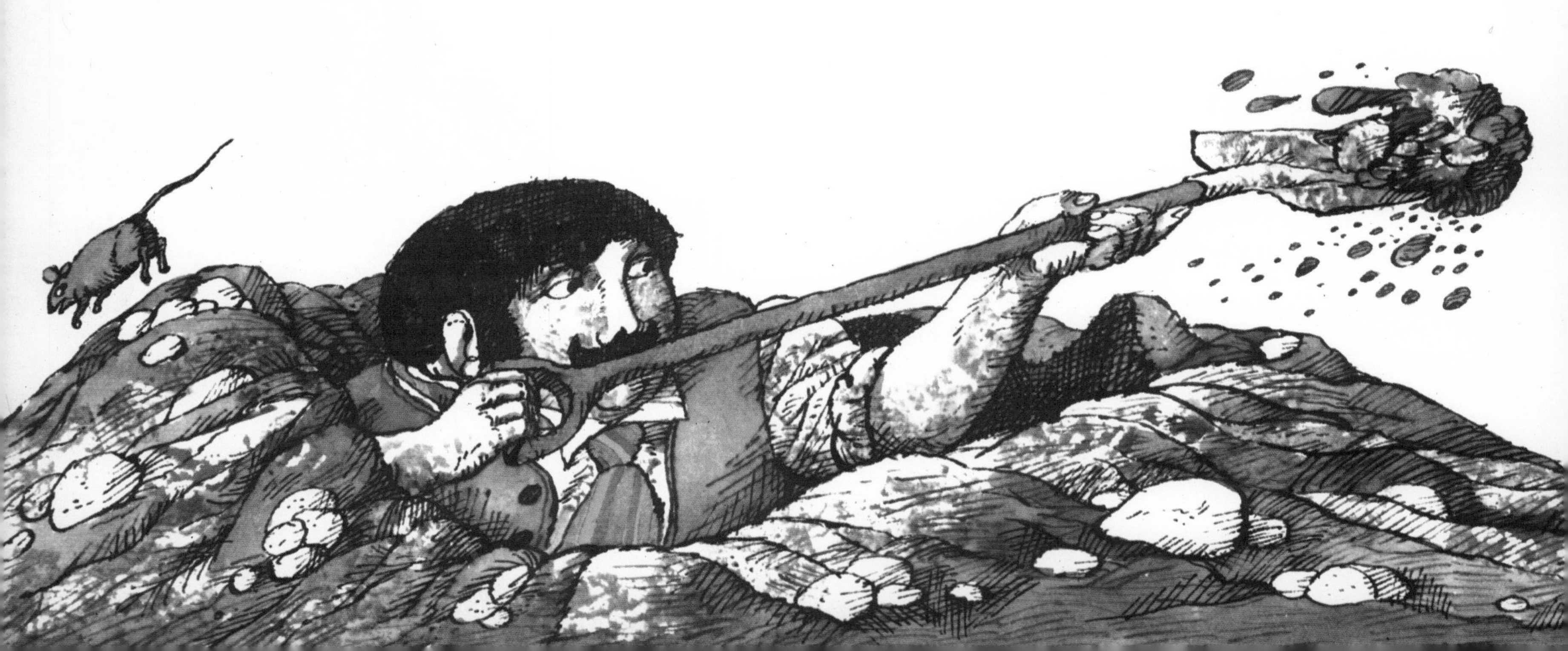

The man, without stopping his digging, said, "Good morning, Your Majesty. As you can see, I'm about to plant a penny bush."

"A penny bush?"

"Oh, yes. You've heard the saying, 'Money doesn't grow on trees.' Well, it grows on bushes. When this hole is deep enough I'll plant a penny in it, and in a few weeks I'll have a nice penny bush."

He drove his spade into the ground. The king growled to Kit, "You are right. He is the biggest dunderhead of all."

At that moment, the man gave a shout. He reached into the hole and pulled out a bag that chinked and clinked. It was full of pennies.

"What luck!" said the man. "I've struck the root of an old penny bush. Now I won't have to plant anything."

And off he ran.

"Great heavens!" exclaimed the king. "Maybe there's something to your school after all. Tell me, can anyone enter?"

"Oh, yes," said Kit. "Come back to my office, and I'll start you on your first class."

Back they hurried together to the city. They went into the house where Kit had hung his sign. There, he showed the king a large wooden box.

"For your first lesson," said Kit, "get into this box."

The king took off his crown and climbed in. Kit closed the lid and locked it.

"Hey!" the king cried. "What are you doing? It's dark and stuffy in here. Let me out!"

SCHOOL
FOR
SILLIES
1st
LESSON

"No, sir," said Kit.
"But when do I learn silliness?"
"You have already learned it, Your Majesty," said Kit. "And I won't let you out until you agree that I have won your daughter."
There was a long silence. Then, "Very well," said the king. "I am beaten."
Kit let him out of the box.

"You have taught me something in your school after all," said the king, sadly. "I now know that instead of being the smartest man in the kingdom, I am as big a fool as anyone else."

"Ah, Your Majesty," said Kit. "That is the beginning of wisdom."

KING KILIAN